WIDE AWAKE WOLF

Georgiana Deutsch

Megan Tadden

LITTLE TIGER

LONDON

It was bedtime in the forest,
but Wolf was wide awake.
He just couldn't sleep!

Wolf tried a
bubbly bath,

and a tasty
bedtime snack.

He even hung
upside down.
But would sleep come?
Not a chance!

It was very strange indeed. "Sleep must be hiding," Wolf declared. "I'll just have to go and find it!" And off he went.

Wolf peered into
a dark den.
"SLEEEEP!
Are you in here?"
he hollered.

Sleep didn't answer,
but Badger did!
"Oof!" he grumped.
"You disturbed
my dream!"

"Sorry," Wolf chattered,
"I'm searching for sleep!
And if you were dreaming,
that means it's only a
whisker away!"

Badger gave a huff. "Well,
we'd better go and find it.
But no more shouting!"

Wolf and Badger hadn't gone far when they heard a lilting lullaby. There, singing softly under the stars, was Hedgehog.

"Sleep is never far from a lullaby!" whispered Wolf. "I'll creep over and catch it!"

"Quickly, then!" grumbled
Badger. "And be QUIET!"
Wolf tiptoed closer,
and closer, until . . .

. . . CRACK
went a crunchy twig.
"EEEK!" yelped Hedgehog.

"Don't be scared!" said Wolf.
"We're just hunting for sleep!
Is it here with you?"

Hedgehog shook her prickles.
"Maybe it's hiding nearby!"
she squeaked.

The friends searched
everywhere, from
dreamy hollows . . .

to the shores of
the moonlit lake.
"I'm exhausted!"
grouched Badger,
and he gave a huge . . .

YAWN!

"Badger — don't move!"
cried Wolf. "Sleep
loves hiding in yawns!"
"In YAWNS?!"
growled Badger.
"That's the silliest
thing I've ever heard!"

"Why don't we ask
Owl?" Hedgehog called.
"I bet she'll know
where sleep is hiding!"

But as they drew near to Owl's tree, they heard a terrible noise. "What's that?" gulped Wolf. "A monster?!" squeaked Hedgehog.

"It's just Rabbit snoring," sighed
Badger. "Obviously!"

But this gave Wolf a bright idea.
"I bet sleep is hiding in Rabbit's
nose," he whispered. "I just
need to tickle it out!"

Wolf found a feather, and . . .

SNUFFLE-SNUFFLE . . . .
SNORT . . .

ATCH

Rabbit hopped off in a huff.
What a kerfuffle!
And **STILL** sleep was
nowhere to be seen.

"OWL!" Wolf howled. "We can't
find sleep ANYWHERE!"

Owl peered down from her moonlit branch. "What's all this about searching for sleep?" she chuckled. "I'm not sure you'll ever find it . . ."

"NEVER find sleep!"
gasped Wolf.
  "Whatever will we DO?"
cried Hedgehog.
  Badger stamped his foot.
"This is Wolf's fault for
scaring it off!" he sulked.

But Owl just smiled kindly. "Sleep will find YOU," she twinkled, "but only when you're tired, and still, and feeling safe. Like when you're listening to a bedtime story."

Wolf thought hard. "Owl?" he blinked.
"Could you maybe tell us a story?"
"Absolutely!" beamed Owl. "Any time!"

The friends snuggled up
under the sparkling stars
while Owl found the
perfect tale.

"It was bedtime in the forest," she began, "but Wolf was wide awake. Tonight, sleep was hiding in the COSIEST place of all . . ."

"...the whispered words of a bedtime story."